MARVEL

IRON MAN

READ-ALONG
STORYBOOK AND CD

This is the story of how Tony Stark became Iron Man. You can read along with me in your book. You will know it is time to turn the page when you hear this sound. . . . Let us begin the story now.

marvelkids.com

Printed in the United States of America

First Edition, June 2017
1 3 5 7 9 10 8 6 4 2
Library of Congress Control Number: 2017931557
ISBN 978-1-368-00959-1
FAC-029261-17111

PLAY TRACK 1 ON YOUR CD NOW!

Anthony "Tony" Stark was an inventor, genius, billionaire, and American patriot. After Tony graduated from college, his parents, Howard and Maria Stark, were killed in a terrible accident. Tony was left in charge of their multibillion-dollar technology company, Stark Industries. Stark Industries was well-known for its development and manufacturing of advanced weapons and defense technologies.

With his unique, brilliant mind, Tony quickly stepped up as chairman of Stark Industries. He invented countless weapons and received numerous awards.

Although Tony was a sharp businessman, he couldn't run the company on his own. He hired an assistant, *Pepper Potts,* who kept him organized and on schedule. *Obadiah Stane,* a friend of Tony's father, stepped in as Tony's mentor and business partner.

Tony enjoyed building weapons and showing them off, but he didn't enjoy the formal events that came with his new job. When he received the esteemed Apogee Award, Tony decided to skip the event. He sent Obadiah to accept the award for him.

"Well, I am not Tony Stark. But, if I were Tony, I would tell you how honored I feel and what a joy it is to receive this very prestigious award. The best thing about Tony is also the worst thing—*he's always working.*"

After the award ceremony, Pepper confronted Tony in his lab.

"You are supposed to be halfway around the world."

Tony was supposed be in Afghanistan presenting his new Jericho missile to a group of high-ranking military officers, alongside his friend and the military liaison to Stark Industries, Lieutenant Colonel James Rhodes. But Tony just smirked at Pepper.

"I thought with it being my plane and all, that it would just wait for me."

***Tony packed up his equipment
and hopped on his personal plane.***
In Afghanistan, he presented his newest
technology to Rhodes and the group of military
men on a ridge that overlooked a vast expanse
of mountains.

"Is it better to be feared, or respected? And I say, is it too much to ask for both? With that in mind, I humbly present the crown jewel of Stark Industries' Freedom line."

Tony signaled toward the mountains and a large missile launched into them. The blast from the impact was so powerful that it blew all the men's hats off!

Tony's audience praised him, and they headed back to the base. But as they were driving, *a huge explosion hit Tony's truck.*

When Tony woke up, he was in a dark cave with a man who called himself Yinsen.

Tony took in his surroundings. Then he looked down. There was a round metal device in the center of his chest, right over his heart. He shot a look at Yinsen.

"What is this?"

Yinsen explained that Tony had been captured and imprisoned by the terrorist group that had caused the car explosion. ***The shrapnel had wounded Tony.*** The metal piece in his chest was an electromagnet keeping him alive.

Suddenly, a menacing man named Raza walked into the cave and demanded Tony build him the Jericho missile. But Tony was never one to be bullied.

"I refuse."

Raza immediately summoned his gang, who forcefully dragged Tony outside the cave. Raza showed Tony that he already had all the equipment Tony would need to build the missile. He wanted him to start work immediately and promised to free Tony once the weapon was delivered.

Tony didn't believe a word Raza said, but he knew he had to build something.

Back in the cave, Tony started assembling, welding, and deconstructing the equipment he was provided. He threw a metal piece behind him.

"Okay, we don't need this."

Yinsen realized that what Tony was building did not look like a missile. Tony pointed at the work in front of him.

"That's because it's a miniaturized arc reactor. I've got a big one powering my factory at home."

Yinsen was very interested in the arc reactor.
He wanted to know the details—how it worked and what it would generate.
Tony enthusiastically explained.

"If my math is right, and it always is, three gigajoules per second."

Yinsen realized that meant the arc reactor could run Tony's heart for fifty lifetimes. Tony shot Yinsen a sideways glance and smiled.

"Or something big for fifteen minutes."

Tony pulled up a blueprint in the cave. It showed his plan to build a metal suit with the arc reactor in the center of its chest plate.
"This is our ticket out of here."
Yinsen believed Tony and decided to help him build the iron suit.

For the next few days, Tony and Yinsen worked on the armored suit around the clock. Finally, it was ready to be fitted.

Tony stepped into the suit and repeated Yinsen's directions to sneak out of the cave. **He had only one shot at getting out.**

"Forty-one steps straight ahead. Then sixteen steps, that's from the door. Fork right, thirty-three steps, turn right."

With a few last-minute adjustments, the suit was activated and Tony escaped from the cave. Raza's henchmen immediately confronted him, but Tony held up his arm, ready to fight.

"My turn!"

In his new armored suit, Tony took down Raza and his men using fire blasts from his arms. Then he rocketed away from Raza's headquarters. But his suit ran out of power and he crashed in the desert miles away, where a military helicopter eventually found him and picked him up.

Tony was welcomed back by Pepper, Obadiah, his supporters, and several news reporters at a press conference.

He addressed the group with his usual wit and charm.

"I came to realize that I have more to offer this world than just making things to blow up. And that is why, effective immediately, I am shutting down the weapons manufacture division. . . ."

The crowd went wild. Cameras snapped and reporters yelled out questions. The news of Stark Industries no longer making weapons was a huge deal.

Outside the press room, Obadiah confronted Tony. He was concerned about Tony's new decision regarding the business, but Tony stood by it.

"We're not doing a good enough job—we can do better, we're gonna do something else. I think we should take another look into arc reactor technology."

Tony opened his shirt and showed Obadiah his own arc reactor.

"It works."

Tony didn't listen to Obadiah's objections and started working on his new initiative, a bigger and better iron suit that would save lives. *For this, he consulted his other assistant, an artificially intelligent computer system named JARVIS.*

"JARVIS, you up? I'd like to open a new project file. 'Til further notice, why don't we just keep everything on my private server. I don't want this winding up in the wrong hands."

Tony worked day and night on his project, spending all his time in the lab with JARVIS. Things got a little tense and Tony snapped at his computer assistant.

"Okay, I'm sorry, am I in your way?"

Pepper grew concerned. She went down to the lab to check on Tony.

"I've been buzzing you. Did you hear the intercom?"

Tony stopped working, looked up, and reassured Pepper that he was fine.

He was just busy building his new suit.

Tony's armor quickly progressed. Soon he had a powerful iron suit with an onboard weapons system! It still needed something to make it look sleek and cool. He rubbed his chin and called out to JARVIS.

"Tell you what, throw a little hot-rod red in there."

Next, Tony concentrated on the jets in his boots and the repulsors in his gauntlets. *He wanted his suit to fly!*

"Activate hand controls."

Tony successfully hovered, but without warning he was thrown across the room. *Test unsuccessful.*

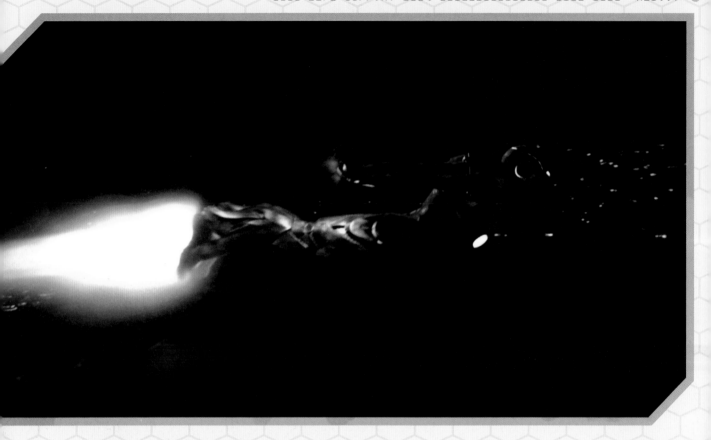

Nothing could stop Tony. He worked harder than he ever had before, and it paid off. He perfected the repulsors in both his gauntlets and boots. He lifted the suit off the ground.

"Yeah, I can fly."

Then he looked over at JARVIS with a grin on his face.

"Sometimes you gotta run before you can walk."

The roof of his lab opened and Tony swiftly took off into the night sky.

He maneuvered the suit like a pro!

He arrived back at his lab. As he went in for a landing, he called out to JARVIS.

"Kill power."

But instead of setting down gracefully, Tony smashed through three floors and into his garage, finally crash-landing right on top of one of his flashy cars!

While Tony continued to improve his suit, he discovered that Obadiah had betrayed their friendship by selling weapons to Tony's enemy, Raza, *and bribing Raza's terrorist group to take Tony's life!*

Tony felt angry and guilty that his weapons were being used to harm others. He flew to the village in his shiny red-and-gold iron suit, armed and ready to take out the bad guys!

When he arrived, he immediately started hitting them with his repulsors, sending the villains crashing into walls. With a final blast from his gauntlets, Iron Man took down the last bad guy and heroically looked up at the villagers.

"He's all yours."

Then he headed back home.

But Tony didn't know that while he was taking down Raza's henchmen and saving the village, Obadiah had hired his own scientists and was secretly working to create *an enormous and powerful iron suit of his own!*

Obadiah instructed his team.

"Set up sector sixteen underneath the arc reactor, and I'm going to want this data masked. Recruit our top engineers. I want a prototype right away."
He specifically directed one of the scientists, "William, here is the technology. I've asked you to simply make it smaller."

He wanted to build his own iron suit to get rid of Tony and take over Stark Industries!

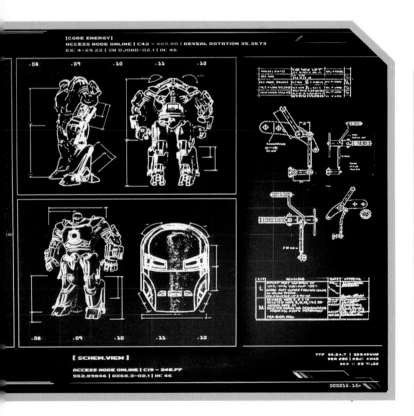

Since Tony knew Obadiah was up to no good, he sent Pepper to hack into his computer and find out exactly what Obadiah had planned. ***Tony soon realized he was going to have to fight his mentor and friend!*** He looked up at Pepper.

"I am gonna find my weapons and destroy them."

Pepper shook her head. "Tony, you know that I would help you with anything, but I cannot help you if you're going to start all of this again."

Tony was upset. ***"There is nothing except this. I just finally know what I have to do, and I know in my heart that it's right."***

Decked out in his red-and-gold armor, Tony took off.

Tony lured Obadiah, who was suited up as the Iron Monger, to the top of the Stark Industries building. He wanted to fight him somewhere no innocent civilians would get hurt. As he attacked the Iron Monger with his repulsors, he shouted commands to JARVIS.

"Divert power to chest RT."

Obadiah slammed Iron Man to the ground and stood over him. "Nothing is going to stand in my way. Least of all you."

Tony once again instructed JARVIS. "Take me to maximum altitude."

The two iron giants threw each other around, until finally Pepper overloaded the large reactor in the lab below them, unleashing a massive electrical surge. The Iron Monger fell into the exploding reactor and was destroyed!

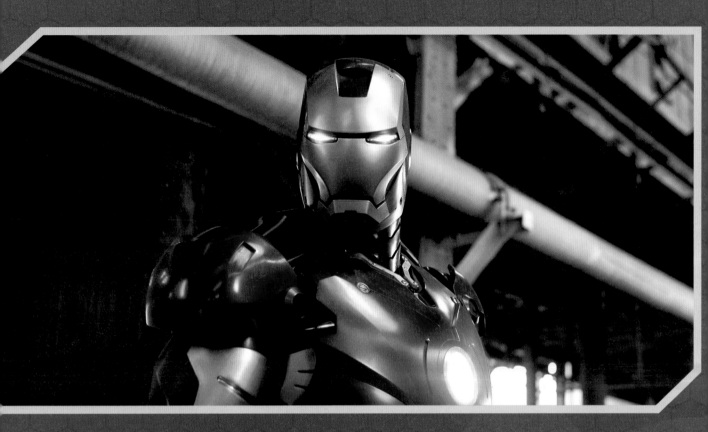

The next day, at a press conference, both reporters and members of the public had a lot of questions about Stark Industries and the iron suits they saw battling in the night sky. One of the reporters referred to the suit as Iron Man.

Tony thought for a moment and turned to his friends.

"'Iron Man.' That's kind of catchy. It's got a nice ring to it. I mean, it's not technically accurate, the suit's a gold-titanium alloy."

Then Tony became serious and addressed the press.

"Truth is...I am Iron Man."

As the room went wild, Tony Stark grinned. He had learned that it was necessary to protect the public. And as the invincible Super Hero Iron Man, he would do just that!

MARVEL STUDIOS

IRON MAN 2

READ-ALONG
STORYBOOK AND CD

This is the story of how Tony Stark defended his Iron Man technology.

You can read along with me in your book. You will know it is time to turn the page when you hear this sound. . . . Let's begin now.

PLAY TRACK 2 ON YOUR CD NOW!

MARVEL

Los Angeles
New York

Tony Stark was a genius and inventor and the CEO of Stark Industries, a multibillion-dollar company known for its development of advanced weapons and defense technologies. At a press conference, Tony had just revealed his biggest secret to the world—his alter ego.

"Truth is . . . I am Iron Man."

Halfway around the world, in Russia, a dying old man named Anton Vanko was watching Tony's press conference. With his last breath, he handed his son, Ivan, blueprints for an arc reactor. The blueprints had Anton's name alongside Tony's father's name, Howard Stark. *This arc reactor was similar in design to the one Tony wore in his chest.* Ivan quickly got to work.

Meanwhile, Tony was enjoying his new identity as Iron Man. He made an appearance at the kickoff of the Stark Expo, which showcased his new technology. But the federal government considered Tony's Iron Man suit a weapon, dangerous to national security, and wanted to confiscate it along with his other technologies. Tony had to appear before the Senate Armed Services Committee, led by Senator Stern.

Tony defended his invention. "I am Iron Man. The suit and I are one. To turn over the Iron Man suit would be to turn over myself. Can't have it."

Stern had no response.

Senator Stern called Justin Hammer, a weapons manufacturer and Tony Stark's business rival, to testify.

Hammer told the committee what it wanted to hear. "In the last six months, Anthony Stark has created a sword with untold possibilities. *And yet he insists it's a shield.* He asks us to trust him as we cower behind it. You know, we live in a world of grave threats, threats that Mr. Stark will not always be able to foresee."

Next, Stern called Lieutenant Colonel James Rhodes to the stand to present his report on the Iron Man suits. Rhodes was Tony's best friend!

Tony was shocked. "Hey, buddy, didn't expect to see you here."
Rhodes shook Tony's hand. "Look, it's me. I'm here. Deal with it. Let's move on."
The committee leader commanded Rhodes to read only a section of his report. Rhodes was angry that his words were going to be taken out of context, but he had no choice. He started reading. "'Iron Man presents a potential threat to the security of both the nation and to her interests.'"

Stern then showed images of other countries attempting to create their own Iron Man suits. According to intelligence, the suits could be operational!

Tony smirked and took over the presentation. "No grave immediate threat here. I'm your nuclear deterrent. It's working. We're safe. America is secure. You want my property. You can't have it. ***But I did you a big favor! I've successfully privatized world peace.***"

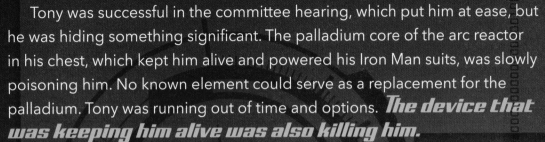

Tony was successful in the committee hearing, which put him at ease, but he was hiding something significant. The palladium core of the arc reactor in his chest, which kept him alive and powered his Iron Man suits, was slowly poisoning him. No known element could serve as a replacement for the palladium. Tony was running out of time and options. *The device that was keeping him alive was also killing him.*

He was having a hard time managing Stark Industries while he tried to figure out the problem with his deteriorating core, so he decided to promote his assistant, Pepper Potts. *"I hereby irrevocably appoint you chairman and CEO of Stark Industries, effective immediately. Take it. Take it."*

"I don't know what to think." Pepper was amazed and accepted the position.

A few days later, Tony and Pepper attended a race in Monaco. One of Stark Industries' cars was competing. Before the race, Tony tested his blood and discovered his palladium levels were high. Feeling reckless, *Tony decided to race the company's car himself!*

Reporters caught him on camera down at the track before the race. He gave them a wave.

The starting flags dropped and Tony raced down the windy track with the other cars. As the lead cars sped around a curve in the road, a man started walking toward them. It was Ivan Vanko! He was wearing a suit with a reactor similar to Iron Man's, with a long electric whip in each hand. **_With a giant crack of one whip, he demolished a race car!_**

As Tony sped around the bend, Ivan cut Tony's race car in two! Tony, unharmed, stood up and fought Ivan. Pepper noticed Tony was in trouble. She had Happy Hogan, Tony's bodyguard, provide him with his Iron Man suit, which enabled him to defeat Ivan. The Russian was taken into custody.

In a Monaco jail, Tony questioned Ivan about the reactor and his Iron Man–like suit. **"Where did you get this design?"** Ivan smirked. He revealed that he had gotten the design from his father, Anton. He told Tony that he wanted to prove to the world that Iron Man wasn't invincible and warned Tony that the world would tear him apart. Tony just laughed at Ivan and left him in his cell.

But Ivan's actions had gained the attention of Tony's rival Justin Hammer.

Hammer helped Ivan fake his own death and escape from jail. ***Hammer wanted Ivan to make a line of armored suits for his company that would be better than Tony's Iron Man suits.*** He planned to showcase them at Stark Expo. Hammer smiled at Ivan. "You and me, we're a lot alike in a lot of ways. The only difference between you and I is that I have resources. I think, if I may, you need my resources, someone behind you, a benefactor. I'd like to be that guy."

After a moment, Ivan agreed to Hammer's deal.

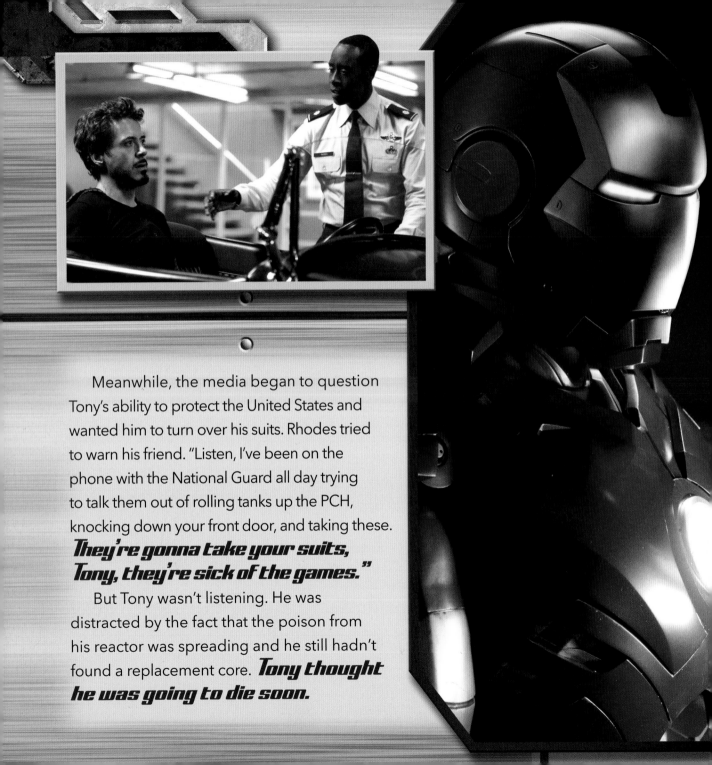

Meanwhile, the media began to question Tony's ability to protect the United States and wanted him to turn over his suits. Rhodes tried to warn his friend. "Listen, I've been on the phone with the National Guard all day trying to talk them out of rolling tanks up the PCH, knocking down your front door, and taking these. **They're gonna take your suits, Tony, they're sick of the games."**

But Tony wasn't listening. He was distracted by the fact that the poison from his reactor was spreading and he still hadn't found a replacement core. **Tony thought he was going to die soon.**

That night, Tony hosted his own birthday party at his house. He wore his Iron Man suit and began to show off its powers to his guests, blasting objects. Rhodes knew he had to stop Tony before he hurt someone. Rhodes put on one of Tony's suits and confronted him. "You don't deserve to wear one of these."

Tony laughed. "Put that thing back where you found it before someone gets hurt."

Rhodes lunged at Iron Man.
The two began to fight! The friends blasted each other with the power of their suits, knocking each other backward and destroying Tony's house. Rhodes shook his head as he looked at Tony and the wreckage, and then he flew off in the silver Iron Man suit, also known as the Mark II. Rhodes delivered the suit to his bosses in the air force. He had to take matters into his own hands.

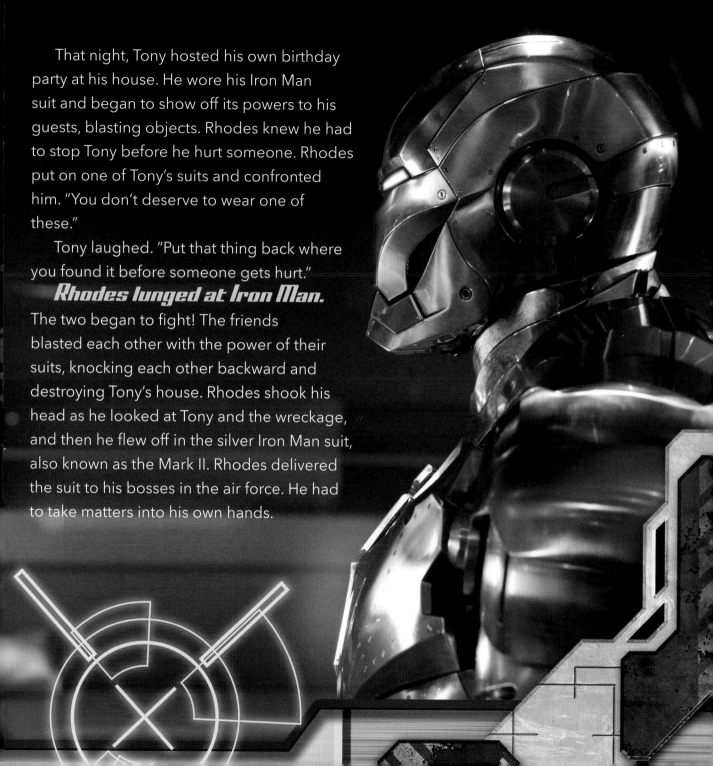

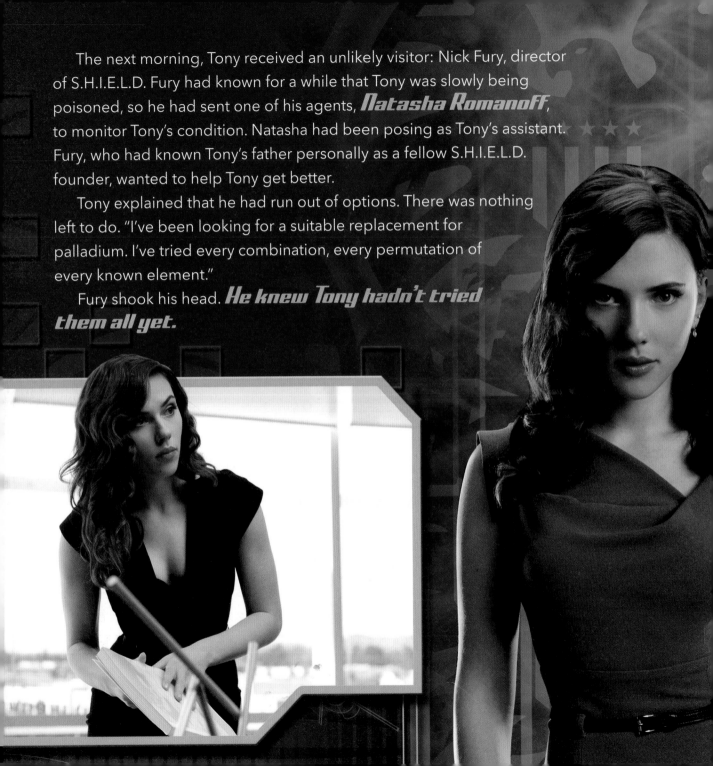

The next morning, Tony received an unlikely visitor: Nick Fury, director of S.H.I.E.L.D. Fury had known for a while that Tony was slowly being poisoned, so he had sent one of his agents, *Natasha Romanoff*, to monitor Tony's condition. Natasha had been posing as Tony's assistant. Fury, who had known Tony's father personally as a fellow S.H.I.E.L.D. founder, wanted to help Tony get better.

Tony explained that he had run out of options. There was nothing left to do. "I've been looking for a suitable replacement for palladium. I've tried every combination, every permutation of every known element."

Fury shook his head. *He knew Tony hadn't tried them all yet.*

Meanwhile, at Hammer's weapons lab, Ivan was working hard on Hammer's new machines. But Hammer was angry when he noticed that Ivan had changed the suit's original design, creating drones. "What is that? That's not a helmet! How are you supposed to get a head in there? I need to fit a person in that suit." How would the suits be able to compete with Iron Man? Ivan shrugged. ***People made mistakes, and his drones would work better.*** Hammer glared at him. "These drones better steal the show, Ivan."

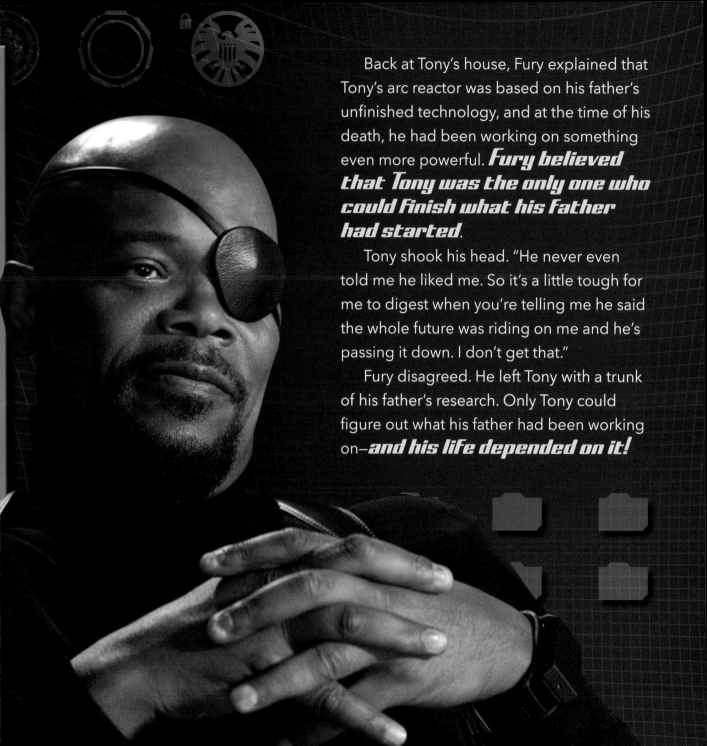

Back at Tony's house, Fury explained that Tony's arc reactor was based on his father's unfinished technology, and at the time of his death, he had been working on something even more powerful. *Fury believed that Tony was the only one who could finish what his father had started*.

Tony shook his head. "He never even told me he liked me. So it's a little tough for me to digest when you're telling me he said the whole future was riding on me and he's passing it down. I don't get that."

Fury disagreed. He left Tony with a trunk of his father's research. Only Tony could figure out what his father had been working on—*and his life depended on it!*

At the air force base, Rhodes's bosses wanted to weaponize the Mark II and use it to make a grand introduction of Justin Hammer's advanced weapons at the Stark Expo.

They brought in Hammer and he presented potential weapons to add to the suit. He also showed them several specialized weapons. Rhodes was skeptical, but he had no choice. *"I think I'll take it. All of it."*

In his lab, Tony watched his father's old videos. In the videos, Howard described the details of the 1974 Stark Expo. Even though Tony had watched the videos on repeat, *he couldn't find any clues.*

Tony needed some air. He went to see Pepper in his old office, but she was angry. "I am trying to run a company. Do you have any idea what that entails? People are relying on you to be Iron Man, and you disappeared." Pepper demanded Tony to leave.

As Tony walked out, he noticed the miniature model of the 1974 Stark Expo in Pepper's office. *He quickly realized that his father might have hidden the secret in it!*

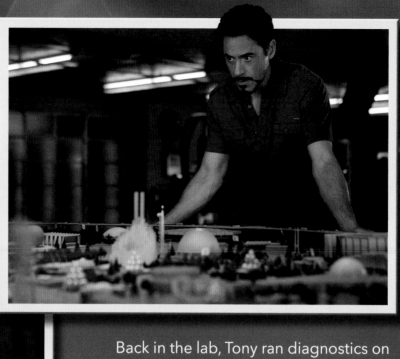

Back in the lab, Tony ran diagnostics on the map. Soon he discovered the structure of a new element in the different features of the expo. Tony smiled at his father's cleverness. *"Dead for almost twenty years. Still taking me to school."*

His artificial intelligence, JARVIS, confirmed that the new element would serve as a replacement for the palladium core. But Tony still needed to synthesize it. He quickly got to work constructing a synthesizer. Soon Tony had created a new element, and his reactor accepted the improved core.

AIR
ASSAULT

GROUND
ASSAULT

On the day of the expo, Hammer was angry. Ivan had promised drones, but they were not ready. Hammer and two of his men confronted Ivan. *"We had a contract! I saved your life, and you give me suits. That was our deal. And you did not deliver."*

Luckily, Hammer had weaponized the Mark II and planned to take credit for the technology. Ivan's drones would be just for show. Hammer left his two guards with Ivan. The Russian smiled slyly. Unbeknownst to Hammer, Ivan had actually managed to make the drones operational *and had a deadly plan for them.*

In no time, Ivan disabled the guards and called Tony to tell him that he planned on hurting his friends. After the call, Stark realized that Ivan was working with Hammer and was planning to attack the Stark Expo!

MILITARY

C387

TACTICAL ASSAULT

961

961

SEA ASSAULT

At the Stark Expo, Justin Hammer revealed his new drones. **"Ladies and gentlemen, today I present to you the new face of the United States military— the Hammer Drone!"**

The crowd was amazed. Then Hammer showed off the weaponized Iron Man suit. "But as revolutionary as this technology is, there will always be a need for man to be present in the theater of war. Ladies and gentlemen, today I am proud to present to you the very first prototype in the variable threat response battle suit and its pilot, Air Force Lieutenant Colonel James Rhodes!"

Suddenly, Iron Man flew in to warn his friend of Ivan's plan. **"We've got trouble. All these people are in danger. We've gotta get them out of here."**

But before Rhodes could do anything, the weapons on his suit pointed at Iron Man. *"I can't move. I'm locked up! Go! This whole system's been compromised!"*

Behind Rhodes, the drones also turned their weapons on Iron Man. From Hammer's lab, Ivan had overridden Rhodes's suit and made the drones operational!

Tony rocketed into the sky as the drones opened fire. A group of drones, led by Rhodes, followed him. Tony tried to override Ivan's control over Rhodes, but he couldn't. All Rhodes could do was shout warnings to his friend. "Tony, on your six!"

Tony wanted to keep the civilians out of harm's way. **"Let's get this away from the expo!"**

Meanwhile, Pepper and Natasha confronted Hammer, who was trying to get control over the drones. He revealed that Ivan was at his facility and was the one behind the attack. Natasha raced off to confront Ivan, but he wasn't there. Natasha found his computer with the drone software and tried to reboot Rhodes's suit and the drones.

Back at the expo, Tony and Rhodes had crashed through a large glass dome. As the two friends fought, Natasha managed to reboot Rhodes's suit. The friends could now fight together to stop Ivan and the drones!

"They're coming in hot, any second." ***Working together, Rhodes and Tony managed to destroy the drones!***

But suddenly, Ivan flew into the dome wearing a large drone suit with electric whips. The two friends fought him, but Ivan was too strong. He managed to trap Tony and Rhodes with his whips.

Tony turned to his friend. "Rhodes. I've got an idea. You want to be a hero? I could really use a sidekick. Put your hand up!"

Tony and Rhodes turned their palms toward each other, sending out energy. The reaction caused a huge explosion. *Ivan was defeated for good!*

Later, Nick Fury paid Tony another visit. Natasha had been evaluating him not only on his health but also on his eligibility for something called the **Avengers Initiative**. Tony accepted Fury's offer to join the initiative, but only as a consultant—with one condition. "Rhodey and I are being honored in Washington, and we need a presenter."

In Washington, Tony and Rhodes smiled as Senator Stern presented them with medals of honor. With Ivan defeated and the problem with his core resolved, Tony's life could go back to normal. **At least for a while . . .**

MARVEL

IRON MAN 3

READ-ALONG
STORYBOOK AND CD

This is the story of how Tony Stark faces off against the Mandarin.

You can read along with me in your book. You will know it is time to turn the page when you hear this sound. . . . Let's begin now.

**PLAY TRACK 3 ON
YOUR CD NOW!**

MARVEL

Los Angeles
New York

Tony Stark was on edge. He had been since his return from helping the Avengers in New York. Instead of sleeping, Tony put all his energy into making more Iron Man suits.

At the same time, America faced a new threat from a man known only as the Mandarin. Tony went to talk to his best friend, Colonel James Rhodes. The colonel served in the air force as the Iron Patriot using one of Tony's suits.

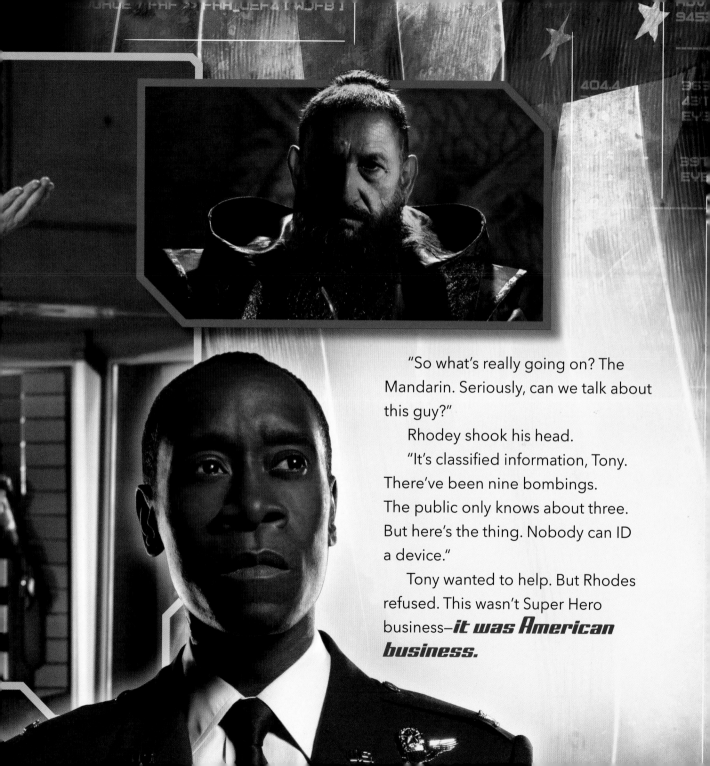

"So what's really going on? The Mandarin. Seriously, can we talk about this guy?"

Rhodey shook his head.

"It's classified information, Tony. There've been nine bombings. The public only knows about three. But here's the thing. Nobody can ID a device."

Tony wanted to help. But Rhodes refused. This wasn't Super Hero business—*it was American business.*

Meanwhile, Tony's girlfriend, Pepper Potts, was busy running Stark Industries. She had a meeting with an old acquaintance of Tony's named Aldrich Killian. His company, AIM, had an idea to pitch.

"It's an idea we like to call Extremis."

Aldrich pulled up an interactive model of the human brain.

"Imagine if you could hack into the hard drive of any living organism and recode its DNA."

Pepper shook her head.

"That would be incredible. Unfortunately, to my ears it also sounds highly weaponizable. *It's gonna be a no, Aldrich.*"

Pepper walked Aldrich out. He and his shady associate, Savin, who had been waiting in the lobby, drove off. Pepper's bodyguard, Happy, was skeptical of the pair. He took a photo of their car's license plate as it sped away.

Happy followed Savin to the Chinese Theater. He watched as Savin handed a briefcase to a mysterious man. Happy bumped into the man, causing the briefcase to spill. When Happy tried to steal one of the metal pieces that had fallen out, he was confronted by Savin. Suddenly, the mysterious man began to glow bright red. *He set off a massive blast in the square!* Happy was knocked unconscious by the impact.

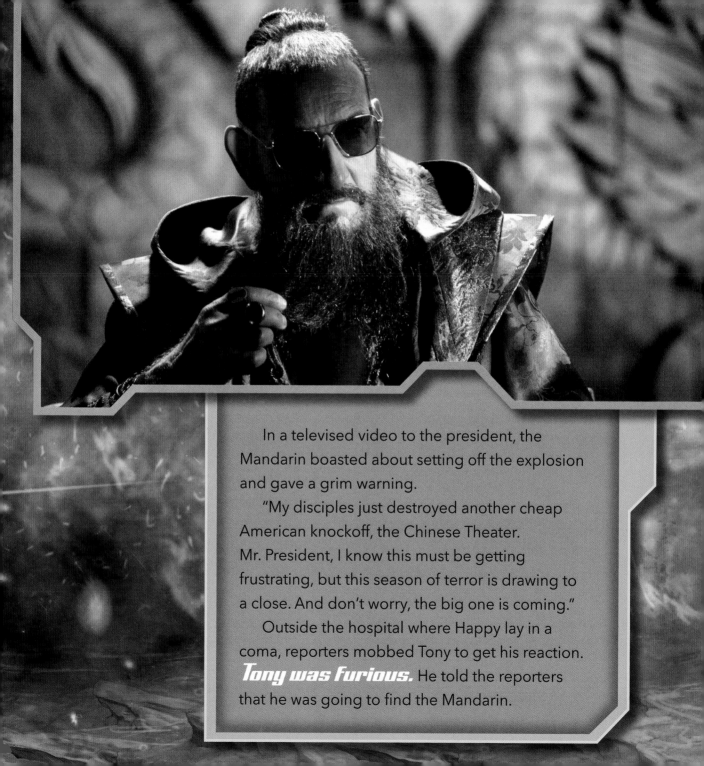

In a televised video to the president, the Mandarin boasted about setting off the explosion and gave a grim warning.

"My disciples just destroyed another cheap American knockoff, the Chinese Theater. Mr. President, I know this must be getting frustrating, but this season of terror is drawing to a close. And don't worry, the big one is coming."

Outside the hospital where Happy lay in a coma, reporters mobbed Tony to get his reaction. **Tony was furious.** He told the reporters that he was going to find the Mandarin.

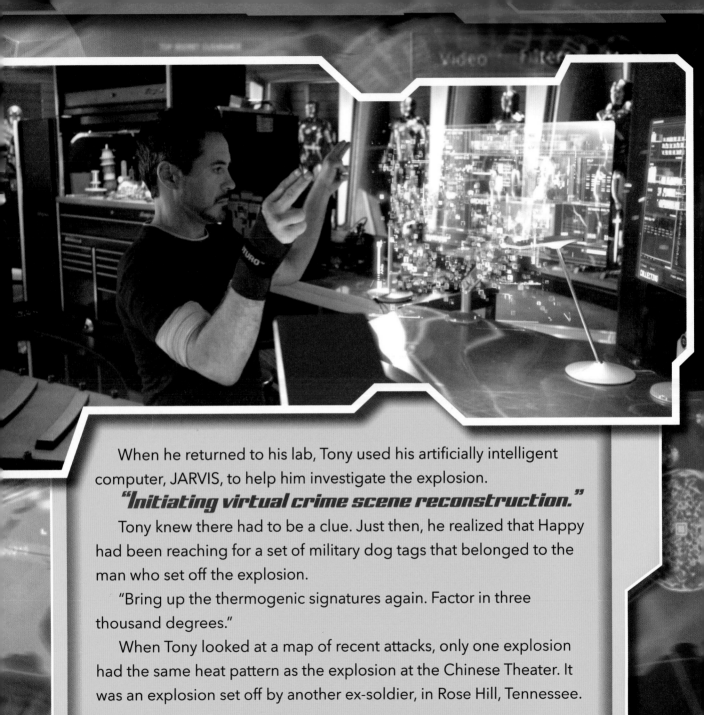

When he returned to his lab, Tony used his artificially intelligent computer, JARVIS, to help him investigate the explosion.

"Initiating virtual crime scene reconstruction."

Tony knew there had to be a clue. Just then, he realized that Happy had been reaching for a set of military dog tags that belonged to the man who set off the explosion.

"Bring up the thermogenic signatures again. Factor in three thousand degrees."

When Tony looked at a map of recent attacks, only one explosion had the same heat pattern as the explosion at the Chinese Theater. It was an explosion set off by another ex-soldier, in Rose Hill, Tennessee.

Before Tony could go investigate, there was a knock at the door. An old friend of Tony's, a scientist named Maya, needed his help. Pepper was annoyed with Tony, and Maya wasn't helping. While Tony and Pepper argued, Maya noticed something headed towards Tony's house. She pointed towards the TV screen. "Do we need to worry about that?" *Just then, a missile hit Tony Stark's house!* The Mandarin's associates had come to destroy Tony. He sent his Iron Man suit to protect Pepper.

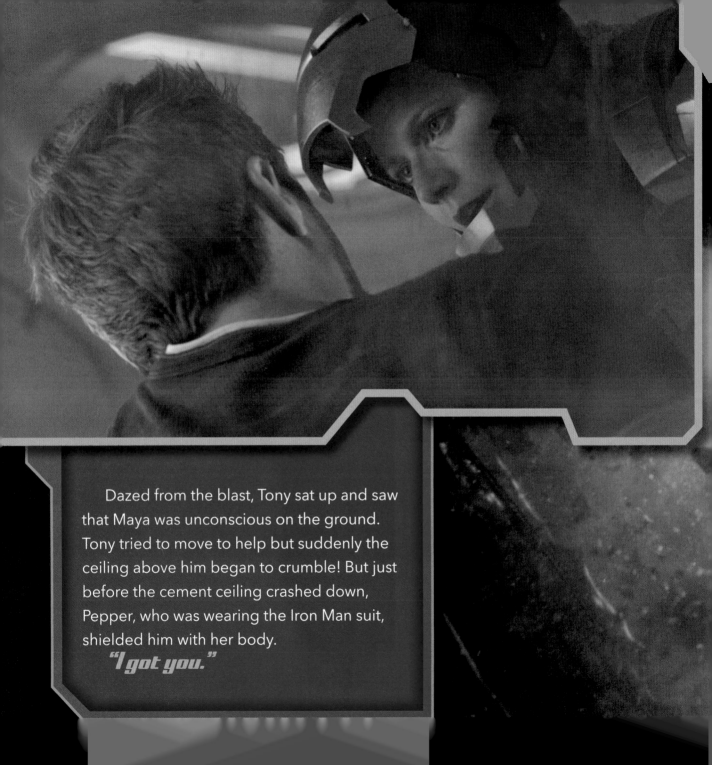

Dazed from the blast, Tony sat up and saw that Maya was unconscious on the ground. Tony tried to move to help but suddenly the ceiling above him began to crumble! But just before the cement ceiling crashed down, Pepper, who was wearing the Iron Man suit, shielded him with her body.

"I got you."

As Pepper and Tony tried to rescue Maya and escape the collapsing building, the floor opened up between them. Pepper was close enough to Maya to get them both to safety. Tony shouted to Pepper over the chaos. "Get her, get outside. Go!"

Pulling Maya with her, Pepper made it to safety as more missiles hit the house. Once they both were safe, Tony called his armor back to him. But the suit was only a prototype and wasn't combat-ready. Tony's house began to crumble, and he fell into the ocean below.

Pepper looked helplessly over the edge. "Tony!"

But he was gone.

When Tony woke, he found himself on a snowy field. His suit had taken the preprogrammed flight path and crash-landed in Tennessee. He left Pepper a message so that she knew he was alive.

"I can't come home yet. I need to find this guy."

Tony knew that he needed to figure out the source of the Mandarin's explosions—and how he could stop him.

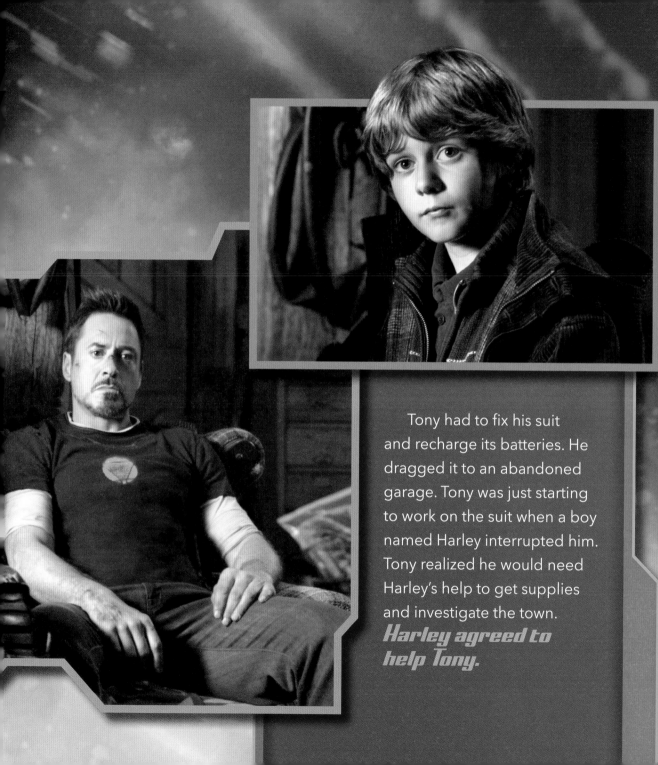

Tony had to fix his suit and recharge its batteries. He dragged it to an abandoned garage. Tony was just starting to work on the suit when a boy named Harley interrupted him. Tony realized he would need Harley's help to get supplies and investigate the town. *Harley agreed to help Tony.*

Tony asked Harley to take him to see the site of the explosion. *Tony surveyed the dark scene.*

"What's the official story here? What happened?"

Harley sat down.

"I guess this guy named Chad Davis used to live aroundabouts. He won a bunch of medals in the army. One day folks said he went crazy."

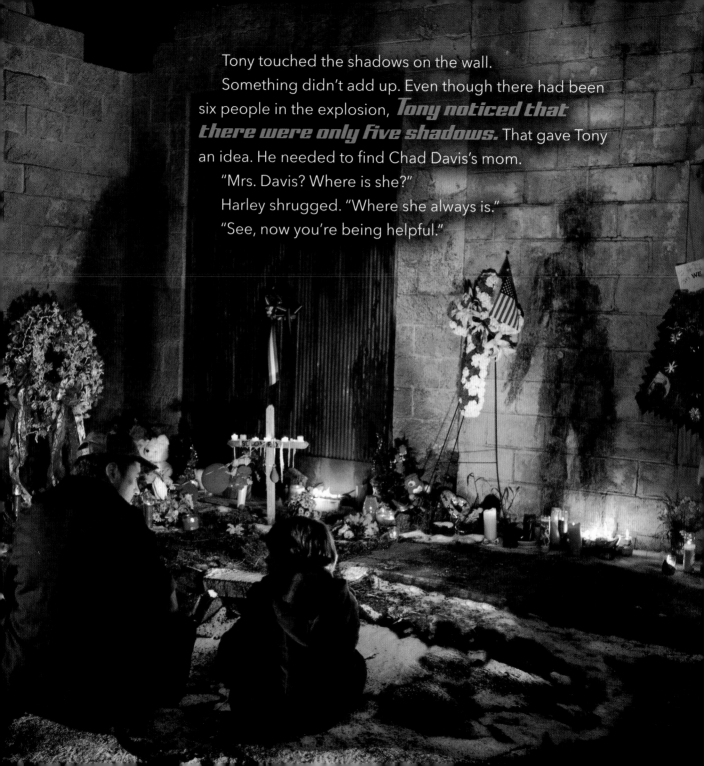

Tony touched the shadows on the wall.

Something didn't add up. Even though there had been six people in the explosion, **Tony noticed that there were only five shadows.** That gave Tony an idea. He needed to find Chad Davis's mom.

"Mrs. Davis? Where is she?"

Harley shrugged. "Where she always is."

"See, now you're being helpful."

Tony found Mrs. Davis inside a restaurant, with her son's file. She mistook Tony for someone she was waiting to meet. Tony flipped through the file. Inside were pictures of several soldiers. Tony recognized one of the names from the dog tags recovered from the Chinese Theater. *All the soldiers looked like they were part of an experiment.*

Suddenly, a female officer arrested Tony. When the local sheriff demanded more information, she started to glow red and attacked! When Tony tried to escape, he saw Savin. He was also glowing red. *The pair both wanted Tony dead and the file destroyed!* Thinking quickly, Tony was able to overcome the Mandarin's two operatives and recover the file.

Tony took a closer look at the project file and discovered it was tied to Aldrich Killian's company—AIM! Tony hacked into AIM's systems and found videos from Killian's Extremis project. Tony realized that the glowing villains were actually wounded soldiers that had been treated with Extremis injections. Some soldiers couldn't handle the injections, causing massive explosions. These explosions are what caused the destruction at the Chinese Theater and the sites of the other Mandarin attacks. *Aldrich Killian was the mad scientist behind the attacks, and Tony knew it.* "This stuff doesn't always work, right, pal? But you found a buyer, didn't you—the Mandarin."

Meanwhile, Maya and Pepper were hiding out in a hotel room. Maya explained that she worked for Aldrich Killian. He had funded her research. She had created Extremis and realized that Killian had sold it to the Mandarin. Just then, Killian barged through the door and grabbed Pepper. He confronted Maya. "So you wanna tell me why you were at Stark's mansion last night?"

An evil smile spread across Maya's face. She wanted Stark to help them launch Extremis. Now that they had Pepper, Tony had an incentive to help them.

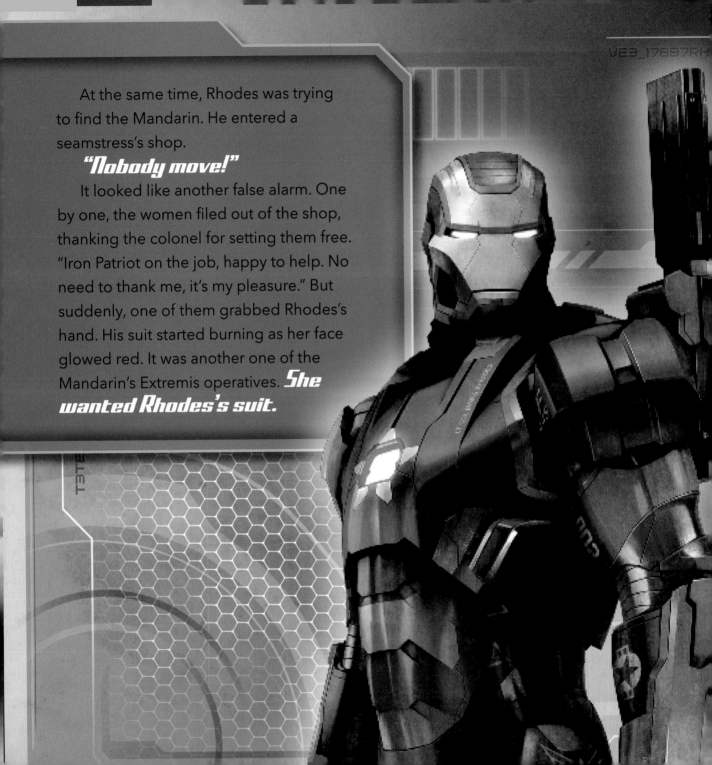

At the same time, Rhodes was trying to find the Mandarin. He entered a seamstress's shop.

"Nobody move!"

It looked like another false alarm. One by one, the women filed out of the shop, thanking the colonel for setting them free. "Iron Patriot on the job, happy to help. No need to thank me, it's my pleasure." But suddenly, one of them grabbed Rhodes's hand. His suit started burning as her face glowed red. It was another one of the Mandarin's Extremis operatives. ***She wanted Rhodes's suit.***

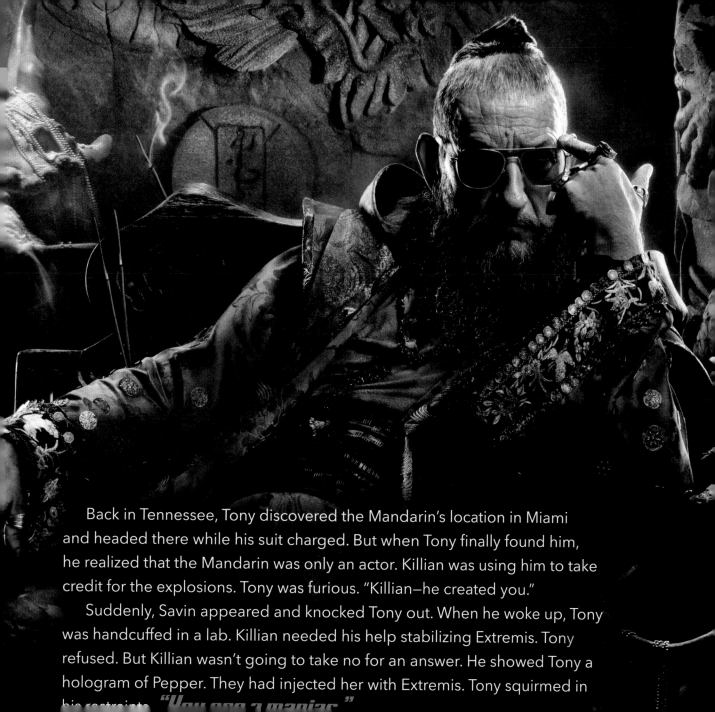

Back in Tennessee, Tony discovered the Mandarin's location in Miami and headed there while his suit charged. But when Tony finally found him, he realized that the Mandarin was only an actor. Killian was using him to take credit for the explosions. Tony was furious. "Killian—he created you."

Suddenly, Savin appeared and knocked Tony out. When he woke up, Tony was handcuffed in a lab. Killian needed his help stabilizing Extremis. Tony refused. But Killian wasn't going to take no for an answer. He showed Tony a hologram of Pepper. They had injected her with Extremis. Tony squirmed in his restraints. *"You are a maniac."*

With Tony restrained, Killian strode to an adjoining room where Rhodes was being held in his Iron Patriot suit. He placed his hand on the suit. The heat from his Extremis powers began pumping through it. *He wanted to use the suit to attack the president.* Rhodes tried to fight him off. "Do not open, don't open."

When he couldn't take the pain any longer, Rhodes fell out of the suit. He tried to fight off Killian, but Savin knocked him out cold.

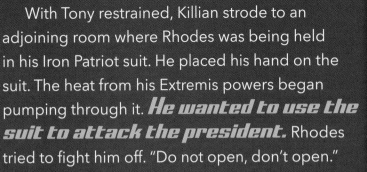

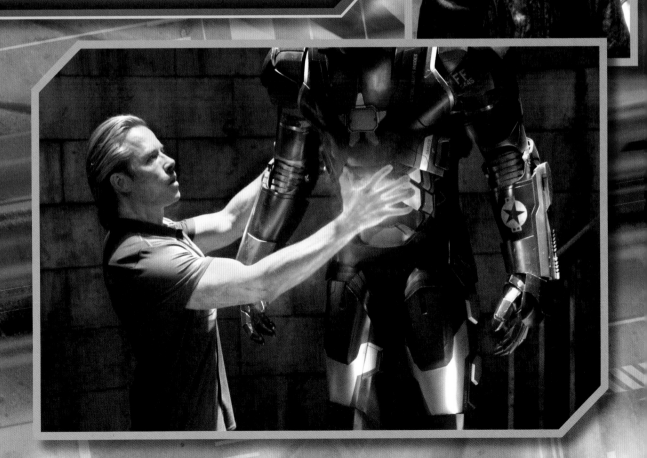

Stuck in the lab, Tony called his Iron Man armor to him. He defeated the guards and met Rhodes in the courtyard. They tried to warn the vice president that the president was in danger on his plane, Air Force One.

"Sir, this is Colonel Rhodes. They're using the Iron Patriot as a Trojan horse. They're gonna take out the president somehow. We have to immediately alert that plane."

The vice president assured Rhodes and Tony that it would be taken care of, but he didn't call anyone. *He was working with Killian!*

On Air Force One, Savin boarded the plane disguised as Colonel Rhodes in the Iron Patriot suit. **_When they were in the air, Savin attacked!_** The Secret Service tried their best to protect the president, but in the Iron Patriot suit Savin was too powerful. With the Secret Service disarmed, Savin grabbed the the president. But the leader wasn't scared. "If you're gonna do it, do it."

Savin opened the Iron Patriot mask and smiled. He had something else in mind. Savin put the president in the Iron Patriot suit and rocketed him out of the plane.

Tony knew time was running out. JARVIS called Tony. He told Tony his Iron Man suit was still only partially repaired and needed more charging.

"The armor is now at 92 percent."

Tony pulled the charging wires from his suit. "That's gonna have to do." **_Tony flew to Air Force One in his suit._** He defeated Savin and saved the crew as the plane plummeted to the ground. But Tony's work wasn't done. He still needed to save the president—and Pepper.

Tony and Rhodes tracked the Iron Patriot armor to an oil rig. Rhodes spotted the president in the Iron Patriot suit.

"Oh my God. He's strung up over the oil tanker. *They're gonna light him up, man.*"

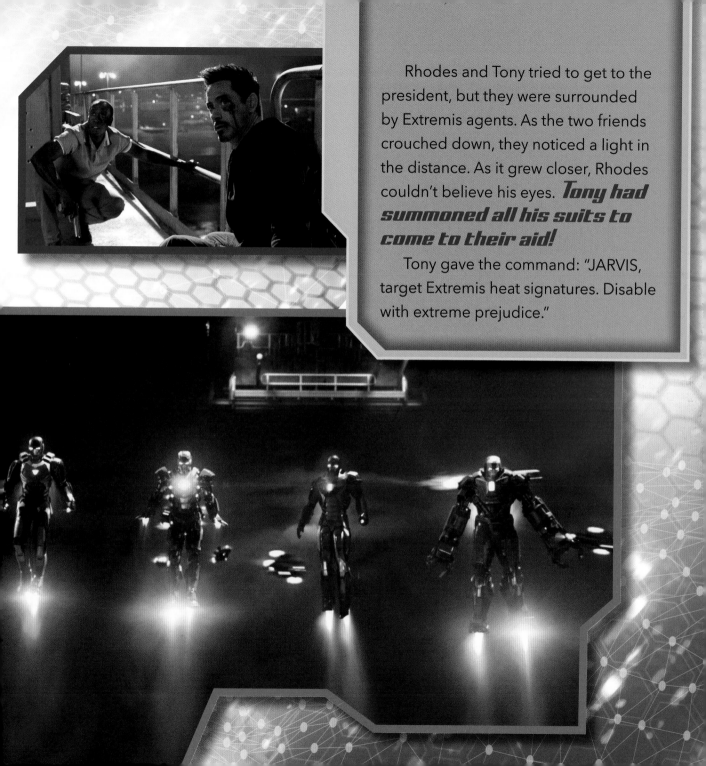

Rhodes and Tony tried to get to the president, but they were surrounded by Extremis agents. As the two friends crouched down, they noticed a light in the distance. As it grew closer, Rhodes couldn't believe his eyes. **_Tony had summoned all his suits to come to their aid!_**

Tony gave the command: "JARVIS, target Extremis heat signatures. Disable with extreme prejudice."

Tony's suits sprang into action, fighting off the Extremis agents. Rhodes hopped onto one of Tony's suits and rescued the president. Tony flew off in his suit to find Pepper. She was buried under a pile of rubble. But as Tony struggled to reach her, Killian appeared! Tony fought him as the rig began to collapse. Pepper was thrown onto a conveyor belt. Tony tried to reach her.

"Honey, you gotta let go. I'll catch you, I promise."

Pepper fell from the conveyor belt, but she slipped through Tony's fingers into the abyss below.

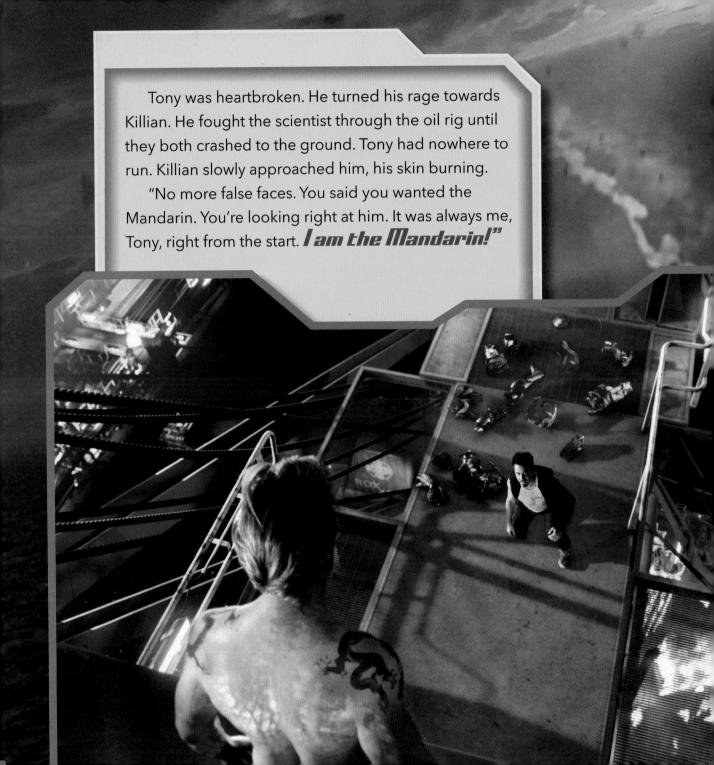

Tony was heartbroken. He turned his rage towards Killian. He fought the scientist through the oil rig until they both crashed to the ground. Tony had nowhere to run. Killian slowly approached him, his skin burning.

"No more false faces. You said you wanted the Mandarin. You're looking right at him. It was always me, Tony, right from the start. *I am the Mandarin!*"

Suddenly, Pepper rose from the flames, knocking Killian away from Tony. She had survived the fall! Taking the arm from one of Tony's suits, Pepper blasted the Mandarin, defeating him!

Tony promised he would get the Extremis out of Pepper. **"That's what I do. I fix stuff."**

Tony wrapped Pepper into a hug, and ordered JARVIS to destroy all of his suits. He was just happy that Pepper was safe.

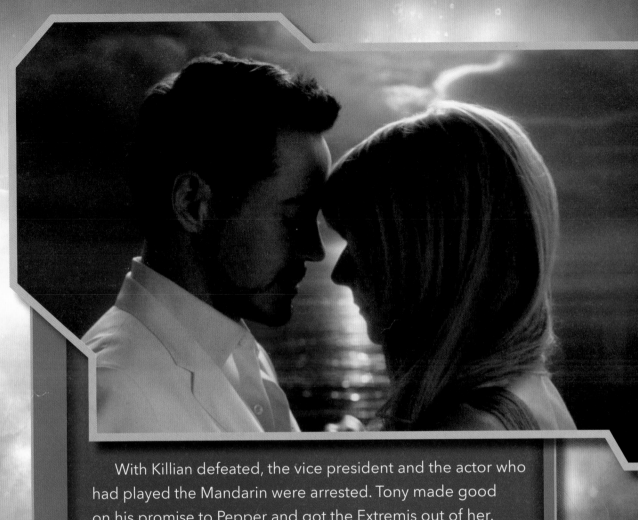

With Killian defeated, the vice president and the actor who had played the Mandarin were arrested. Tony made good on his promise to Pepper and got the Extremis out of her. Happy woke from his coma, and Tony sent Harley presents for helping him. He thought about everything that he had been through as he looked out over the wreckage of his home.

"My armor, it was never a distraction, or a hobby. It was a cocoon. And now I'm a changed man. You can take away my house. All my tricks and toys. *One thing you can't take away: I am Iron Man.*"